TEEN
HOT LINE

AIDS

Barbara Lerman-Golomb

RSVP
RAINTREE
STECK-VAUGHN
PUBLISHERS
The Steck-Vaughn Company

Austin, Texas

Consultants:
Scott Moyer, Consortium Coordinator, Mercer County HIV Consortium, Trenton, NJ
William B. Presnell, American Association for Marriage and Family Therapy

Developed for Steck-Vaughn Company by Visual Education Corporation, Princeton, New Jersey
Project Director: Paula McGuire
Editors: Jewel Moulthrop, Linda Perrin
Photo Research: Sara Matthews

Raintree Steck-Vaughn Publishers staff
Editor: Kathy Presnell
Project Manager: Julie Klaus
Electronic Production: Scott Melcer
Photo Editor: Margie Foster

Library of Congress Cataloging-in-Publication Data
Lerman-Golomb, Barbara.
        AIDS / Barbara Lerman-Golomb.
             p.   cm. — (Teen hot line)
        Includes bibliographical references and index.
        ISBN: 0-8114-3814-7
        1. AIDS (Disease) — Juvenile literature.   [1. AIDS (Disease)]
    I. Title. II. Series.
        RC607.A26L465   1995
        616.97′92— dc20   94-30055
                                                                                      CIP
                                                                                      AC

Photo Credits: Cover: © David Young-Wolff/PhotoEdit; **14:** © Phillip Wallick/Photo Network; **17:** © Robert Brenner/PhotoEdit; **22:** © Rosenthal/Superstock; **26:** UPI/Bettmann; **31:** © Shirley Zeiberg; **35:** © Michael Keller/PhotoEdit; **41–48:** UPI/Bettmann; **53:** © Ryan Nolan/Leo deWys; **66–72:** UPI/Bettmann; **73:** © Elena Rooraid/PhotoEdit.

Printed and bound in the United States

1 2 3 4 3 5 6 7 8 9 0 LB 99 98 97 96 95

CONTENTS

What the

Teen

Hot Line

Is All About

This book is like a telephone hot line. It answers questions about AIDS that may be confusing you. Answering your questions requires us to give you the facts about the HIV virus, how it is transmitted, and how it develops into AIDS over time. You can use these and other facts to make your own decisions about engaging in risky behavior or to better understand what it means to be HIV-positive, or to have AIDS, or to be in contact with people with AIDS. So think of us as the voice on the phone, always there to answer your questions, even the ones that are difficult for you to ask.

To help you deal with this subject, here is a list of seven steps we think a person should take to understand the disease and reduce the risks of getting AIDS. These steps focus on finding out facts and using common sense. They assume that you want to make your own decisions and act responsibly both toward yourself and others.

1 By reading this book and other sources, find out everything you can about AIDS: what it is, who can become infected, and how it is transmitted.

2 Talk to people who can give you the information you need to separate the rumors from the truth about AIDS. These can include friends, parents, your family doctor, and other adults in whom you can confide.

3 Consider carefully the kinds of risky behavior or situations that can result in contracting the AIDS virus.

4 Understand that anyone who does not avoid risky behavior may become infected with HIV.

5 Learn about how the spread of the AIDS virus can be prevented.

6 Learn how individuals and society deal with the disease and the lack of a cure.

7 Understand your responsibility toward the people around you and make some vital decisions about your future behavior.

After you read this book, we hope you will have some answers to your questions about AIDS and perhaps to some questions you hadn't thought of yet. At the back of the book is a list of sources for further information. Thinking now about the issues raised in this book may make a profound difference in your life.

Interview

Billy, now 17, was in a car accident when he was seven years old. By the time he got to the hospital, he had lost a lot of blood, and he had to receive a blood transfusion. This was in 1984, one year before there was mandatory screening of blood for HIV antibodies. Eight years later, he lost weight and began feeling unusually tired. He also developed swollen lymph glands. When ordinary tests for these symptoms showed no cause, the doctor finally tested Billy for the HIV virus. The test was positive. With no other risk factor apparent, the doctor could only guess that the blood used in Billy's earlier transfusion had been contaminated with the HIV virus. Like many people with the HIV virus, he had shown no signs of illness for many years. Then, suddenly, he showed symptoms of someone with HIV disease. He had not yet, however, contracted one of the infections that signals full-blown AIDS, or the last stage of the HIV disease.

I was banged up pretty badly when I was in the car accident. I had to miss school for six months. It was really hard on my family, but we got through it okay, and luckily I didn't have any lasting injuries or problems.

Then about eight years later when I was fifteen, I began feeling lousy. My family doctor wanted me to come in for some tests. That was a really strange day, because I hadn't been in that hospital since I was a little kid. It brought back a lot of scary memories for me.

Anyway, a couple of weeks later the doctor called. I answered the phone. He said he wanted to talk to my mom or dad. When my mom hung up the phone, she looked upset. But she wouldn't tell me what was wrong. I thought right then that the doctor had told her something awful about me. But I found out later that he hadn't told her anything. He waited until he could talk to my parents in person. Then it was their turn to tell me.

I was doing some homework and listening to music on my headphones when they came into my room. They sat down on my bed on either side of me. They started to talk even before I had pulled the headphones off my ears. That's how they told me I was HIV-positive. I thought they were crazy at first. People like me didn't get AIDS. But I was wrong. People like me do get AIDS. I started thinking back to what I learned about AIDS in health class at school. I remembered teachers telling us about how people get it through unprotected sex, IV drugs, and blood transfusions. And even though I had had a transfusion when I was younger, it didn't register that this could happen to me.

There were a couple different things my parents and I did right away. We met with my doctor to talk about the physical side of AIDS—what was going to happen to me, how I could try to keep from getting sicker. Then he told us the name of a family counselor we could talk to.

Meeting with the counselor has helped all of us in different ways. For one thing, it's taught us not to be so angry or to look for someone to blame for my illness. That was hard for my parents at first, because they felt that somehow it was their fault. The counselor has also helped me to think more positively and to see the good things in life. She's put me in touch with a support group for teenagers with HIV, and I've made some good friends. That's the good part of being in the group. The bad part is when someone in the group gets really sick.

My parents and I did a lot of reading about AIDS. We found out how you could or couldn't pass on the virus to other people. In the beginning, even after they knew how you could get it, they ran all of my dishes and silverware through the dishwasher to make sure any germs were killed. But now they know that you can't get the virus just from touching stuff that an infected person has touched.

My school's been cool about me being there. But there are still people I meet who are nervous about shaking my hand, borrowing a pen from me, or using the pay phone after I've been on it. I'm lucky, though, because my friends still want to be around me. I've missed some days of school because I've been sick. But I'm planning on graduating next year and maybe even going on to college.

I think there's still a problem with the way people with AIDS are treated. And, it seems like if you got HIV through sex or sharing needles, you're treated differently than if you got it through contaminated blood. It's like people can only think of you in two ways: you're either a bad person or a victim. I don't want anybody to think of me as a victim. I just want people to treat me normally and be decent to me.

BULLETIN BOARD

The first cases of AIDS were diagnosed in 1981.

An estimated 1 million Americans have been infected with HIV.

About four million women give birth in the United States each year. Disease centers estimate that 6,000 to 7,000 of them are HIV-infected. About 1,500 to 2,000 of their babies will be HIV-infected.

In the United States, over 250,000 people have been diagnosed as having AIDS.

Among adolescents and young adults (age 13 to 24), 10,528 cases of AIDS have been reported. Because the time between becoming infected with HIV and developing AIDS can be 10 years or more, many people with AIDS who are in their twenties (currently 1 of 5 reported cases of AIDS) were infected while they were teenagers.

Over 170,000 people in the United States have died of AIDS. That's nearly three times the number of Americans who died in the Vietnam War.

In 1991, HIV infection and AIDS was the sixth leading cause of death among people 15 to 24 years old in the United States.

AIDS is now one of the three main causes of death for women and men ages 25 to 44.

Every day, more than 100 people in the United States die of AIDS, or 1 every 15 minutes.

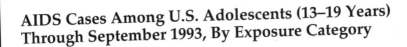

AIDS Cases Among U.S. Adolescents (13–19 Years) Through September 1993, By Exposure Category

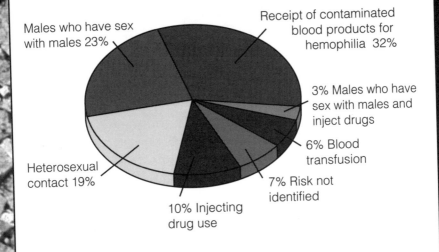

Males who have sex with males 23%

Receipt of contaminated blood products for hemophilia 32%

3% Males who have sex with males and inject drugs

6% Blood transfusion

7% Risk not identified

10% Injecting drug use

Heterosexual contact 19%

Source: *Facts About Adolescents and HIV/AIDS,* CDC National AIDS Clearinghouse, October, 1993.

Sources:

The Alan Guttmacher Institute.

Centers for Disease Control and Prevention, Division of HIV/AIDS.

The Center for Population Options.

National Committee on AIDS (NCOA). Americans Living with AIDS. NCOA, 1991.

Sexual Activity

Average age of first sexual intercourse: 16

% of females who have had sexual intercourse by age 16: 34

% of males who have had sexual intercourse by age 16: 50

% of all teens who use condoms: 45

% of teens with multiple sex partners who use condoms: 41

One in four 12th graders reported having four or more sexual partners in a 1990 study.

Communicating

Q My name is Cara. It seems like all anybody ever talks about these days is AIDS. The thing is, the more I hear about it, the more confused I get. It's not the easiest thing to talk about. So, what can I do to get some answers?

A You're not the only one who's confused, Cara. AIDS is still a mystery to many people. But it's really important to get the facts, to understand as much as possible about the disease, and to know how to protect yourself. Luckily, there are a lot of different sources to help you out—your school guidance counselor, your family doctor, your health teacher, telephone hot lines, and books. It's also important to talk to your parents. Even though they may not have all the answers, they might direct you to someone who does.

. . . .

Q Talk to my parents? Get real. If I start asking them questions about AIDS, they'll think *I've* got it. They'll also probably start asking me a lot of embarrassing questions about my boyfriend and sex. How am I supposed to handle that?

A Think about it this way. Wouldn't your parents want you to know how to protect yourself against HIV rather than put yourself at serious risk? Remember, being embarrassed only lasts a few minutes, but HIV and

AIDS never go away. However, if you can't talk to your parents, then talk to another adult.

• • • • • • • • • • • •

 I guess you're right. But I'm not even sure how to get the conversation started. And, I don't want to look stupid by asking a dumb question.

A Keep in mind that there are no stupid questions when it comes to talking about AIDS. Any question that might save a life is a good question. But if you want to feel more comfortable before talking to someone, it might help to prepare some questions that you may have about AIDS.

• • • • • • • • • • • •

Sorting It All Out

There are many reasons why AIDS is such a difficult subject to talk about. One reason is that it often involves talking about sex. Sometimes this can make you feel uncomfortable, especially when you're talking to a parent or another adult. Other reasons include the possibility of having to talk about homosexuality, drugs, or even someone you know who's infected with the AIDS virus—subjects that may be difficult to bring up easily in conversation. It's a scary subject, one you may have avoided until now.

To put both you and the person you're speaking with at ease, approach the subject in an organized manner. Bring along a list of all the things you've heard about AIDS. As you talk and get more information, put a check mark next to anything that's true. There are a lot of rumors and misinformation out there, and you need to be able to separate what's fact and what's fiction.

HIV/AIDS and the World

- [ ] As of January 1992, 10–12 million people, including 1 million children, were infected with HIV.

- [ ] The World Health Organization (WHO) predicts that AIDS will soon be the leading cause of premature death in many Western cities; up to 10 million African children will be orphaned by AIDS by the end of the 1990s.

- [ ] About 90 percent of new infections are the result of heterosexual transmission.

- [ ] By the year 2000, the total number of cases may rise to 40 million, of which 90 percent will be in sub-Saharan Africa, South and Southeast Asia, Latin America, and the Caribbean.

- [ ] On a worldwide basis, 70 percent of those infected are female.

- [ ] WHO estimates that 2 million cases of AIDS have occurred since the beginning of the epidemic.

Source: *Current and Future Dimensions of the HIV-AIDS Pandemic* (WHO document).

If something is confusing, don't be embarrassed to ask more questions about it until you really understand that particular issue. AIDS is an illness that involves complicated medical terms that will be unfamiliar to you.

By approaching the subject in a mature way, you'll be showing the adult you're talking to that you want to be treated responsibly. This will pave the way for other serious discussions you may want to have in the future.

Avoiding Misinformation

AIDS was first identified in the United States in 1981. We may never know where or how the disease began. Many researchers believe it had been in the United States, Europe, and Africa for several decades before the first cases were identified. It was associated in the beginning with only a few groups of people. These included homosexual men and intravenous (IV) drug users (people who inject drugs into their veins). As more people were diagnosed, these groups soon also included bisexual men, hemophiliacs (people with blood diseases that require frequent transfusions), and immigrants from Haiti and Central Africa. Today the number of newly diagnosed cases of AIDS is going down among homosexual men because of safer sex practices, but it is rising among drug users and heterosexual men and women.

AIDS has become an epidemic. It is, in fact, a pandemic since it exists all over the world. It has been found in almost every

It is important for you to find out all you can about AIDS. Discussing it with an informed teacher or guidance counselor is a good way to get the facts and avoid misinformation.

group in the U.S. population, including children. It is recognized that *anyone who does not avoid high-risk behavior can contract the AIDS virus.* Currently, AIDS is fatal; as of yet there is no known cure for the disease.

Until medical researchers find some way to control the spread of the disease, it is the responsibility of every individual to face up to the possibility that he or she is a potential patient. Teenagers, especially, who are involved in so many dynamic and exciting physical and emotional changes at this time in their lives, need to stop and examine the serious facts about AIDS. It is easy for them to think they are invincible to misfortune, accident, or illness, and so they may take needless risks without regard to the consequences. Don't fall into the trap of thinking it can't happen to you. It has already happened to hundreds of teenagers. Take charge of your life, and make sure you preserve it.

Taking Control of Your Life

One of the biggest decisions many teenagers face is whether or not to become sexually active. Since AIDS has become such an urgent problem, this decision has taken on even more importance. Before making your decision, learn all you can about AIDS. Be sure you understand that the only foolproof way to remain free of becoming infected with AIDS through sexual contact is to abstain from having sexual intercourse.

Pete, age 16, started dating Jillian four months ago. Jillian, also 16, was new to the high school. Before Pete, she had dated a 20-year-old friend of her brother's. Jillian told Pete that she had been sexually active with this other guy. And, as a matter of fact, he hadn't been the first one. When Pete heard this, he called the Hot Line because he was worried.

"I don't want Jillian to think I don't care about her, and I don't want her to break up with me. But I'm scared she might be infected with HIV. How can I tell her that?"

Pete knew that he had to talk the situation through with Jillian, but he feared what her reaction would be. His fears about AIDS grew even stronger, however, so he worked out a strategy for bringing up the subject with her. He told her in advance he wanted to talk privately about something important with her and made a date for the next weekend. Then he practiced in advance what he would say.

Pete was able to speak honestly with Jillian. He told her of his concern about contracting the HIV virus and that he would be uncomfortable having a closer physical relationship with her. He let her know, in fact, that he had made up his mind not to be sexually active with anyone for the time being. He suggested she think about it and consider continuing their relationship on that basis.

Jillian was really surprised that Pete took the subject so seriously. She had taken sex for granted with her former boyfriend, perhaps because he was older. She admitted being worried about it now, however, and decided to be tested for HIV. Jillian valued Pete's openness and looked forward to continue building a caring relationship with him.

Confronting the Problem

Take a lesson from Pete. If you need to discuss a problem with someone close, there are some steps you can take to make it easier for both of you:

■ Let the person know you want to discuss something important and arrange for a quiet time together. Don't catch someone off guard and spring a problem without warning.

■ Know how you feel and what you want to say in advance. Think through how you will present what you want to say. Stay calm, and simply state facts and your feelings, so that the other person does not feel accused of doing something bad.

Sometimes you may feel more comfortable discussing your questions about sexual activity or other risky behavior with a friend rather than with an adult. An open exchange about HIV may help you make important decisions about your life.

■ When it's the other person's turn to talk, listen carefully. When two people are really listening to each other, it's easier to resolve the problem between them.

Making Your Decision

The decision you make now about your sexual behavior may be the most important one you ever make. If you are already sexually active or considering becoming so, you need to talk to your partner. You'll probably discover that he or she is just as scared and confused as you are. If your partner is pressuring you to have sex, he or she may not be the right person for you to be spending time with. Remember, no one else can tell you how you feel or what you should do. Not being involved sexually, however, doesn't mean that this has to be the end of your relationship. Talk about it and decide if it's worth the risks. If you still feel you want to be sexually active, find out everything you can about AIDS immediately.

If abstinence is your choice of behavior:

■ Don't be talked out of it.

■ Don't put yourself in situations where it may be difficult to stick to your decision. Try not to spend all your time alone with your partner. Plan activities with groups of friends.

■ Stay away from drugs and alcohol. They can affect your judgment, your inhibitions, and your behavior.

■ Keep lines of communication open at all times.

Having worked through a difficult decision both rationally and emotionally may have been hard. But once you've done it, you will have learned a skill you can use the rest of your life.

Knowledge Is Power

Q A guy on our school football team has something called HIV, which is supposed to be like AIDS. Now I'm worried about playing with him. I mean, what if he gets cut and some of his blood gets on me? Or, what if he's sweating, or if he coughs or sneezes? Isn't it dangerous for me and the other guys on the team to be around him?

A Your question brings up the problem of myths about HIV and AIDS. Before you and the other guys start taking matters into your own hands, I think you ought to talk to your coach. Maybe suggest to him or her that it would be a good idea if the whole team sat down to discuss their feelings about playing with someone who is HIV-positive. And, before you jump to conclusions, get the facts.

• • • • • • • • • • • •

What Does It All Mean?

AIDS has become a household word, but how many people really understand what it means? Here's what it stands for: Acquired Immunodeficiency Syndrome.

A: Acquired
  This is something you get or can develop.
I: Immuno
  This refers to the body's immune system, which keeps us from getting certain infections, diseases, and cancers.

D: Deficiency
   This is a lack of (not enough of) something.
S: Syndrome
   This is a group of symptoms that show something is wrong.

AIDS is caused by a virus called HIV—Human Immuno-deficiency Virus. A virus is a living organism that causes various diseases. Different illnesses are caused by different viruses. For example, being sick with the flu is sometimes referred to as "having a virus." Just as the flu is caused by the flu virus, AIDS is caused by the HIV virus. To be HIV-positive means that a person's blood tested positive for the presence of HIV. In other words, HIV was found in the blood system.

We have certain cells in our bodies that create an immune or defense system—keeping us healthy and protecting us from germs that can enter our bodies. The immune system works to keep us from getting sick and also helps us to recover if we *do* get sick.

Here's one way to picture this. Imagine a video game called *Attack!* In this game, there is a row of giant creatures at the top of the screen. They are lined up like a wall, protecting rows and rows of smaller creatures below them. Suddenly, mutant aliens drop from a spaceship and attack all the creatures. If the giant creatures can't defend themselves, the aliens gobble them up—destroying their protective wall. This leaves the remaining smaller creatures open to attack by the aliens. Eventually, when the wall disappears, all the creatures are destroyed, and the game is over.

In the case of AIDS, the HIV virus attacks and eats away at special white blood cells—T-lymphocytes or T-cells (sometimes called T4-cells or CD4 cells)—that have been protecting a person like a wall. Once those cells are destroyed in the body, the immune system is weakened, and the person is open to getting various infections and diseases. These infections are called *opportunistic infections* because they find an opportunity to enter the body in its defenseless state. The virus begins to multiply, reproducing more and more of the AIDS virus, which eventually kills the white blood cells altogether.

The immune system will keep trying to work even after some cells are destroyed. This means that it may take a while until symptoms begin to show up—as long as eight to ten years, in some cases. It all depends on the person who is infected. The number of T-cells in a person's blood shows how strong his or her immune system is. A normal T-cell count is between 800 and 1,200. Health care providers recommend that a person who is HIV-positive have his or her T-cell count checked every six months or sooner, depending on the count. Under the definition by the CDC (Centers for Disease Control), people with a T-cell count of under 200 are considered to have AIDS. (But there are in fact some people walking around with extremely low T4-cell counts who have been able to avoid the major illnesses associated with AIDS. Many scientists are baffled by this.)

According to the CDC, there are 26 AIDS-related illnesses. A person who has one of these illnesses is considered to have AIDS. After contracting one of these illnesses, most patients die in two to three years. In many cases, a person with AIDS may recover from one infection only to have another a few months later. With each new infection, the patient becomes weaker and weaker and is less able to do normal everyday activities.

How the Virus Is and Is Not Spread

The biggest myth about HIV is that you can get it through casual contact. Here's the reason why this is not true:

The AIDS virus cannot survive well outside of the body, and human skin presents an effective barrier to it.

In fact, what makes the AIDS virus different from most other viruses is that it cannot contaminate air, food, or water.

Here's what you should know about how HIV is not transmitted.

A person cannot get HIV from:

■ Cough or sneeze droplets in the air, or sweat

■ Swimming pools, showers, locker rooms, towels, bathtubs, or toilet seats

■ Holding hands, hugging, touching, shaking hands

■ Closed mouth or "social" kissing

■ Casual contact: Being around an infected person at work, home, or school; touching things an infected person has used such as silverware, drinking glasses, and plates; or sharing food

Casual contact, such as holding hands, is a safe way for couples to display affection.

■ Being in a crowd, eating in public areas (restaurant, school cafeteria), using a public restroom, water fountains, doorknobs, public telephones

■ Mosquito bites, donating blood

Making Contact

If you know someone who is HIV-positive or has AIDS, you may have some fears about being in close contact with him or her. Here's a fact that may take away your fears. The AIDS virus does not live in mucus (secretions) in your nose or throat. This means AIDS cannot be transmitted by having an infected person sneeze or cough near you. Also, very little or no AIDS virus has been found in the teardrops, saliva, and sweat of infected people. Even if there were traces of the virus in these fluids, it wouldn't be enough to cause infection.

Since the AIDS virus cannot survive once it comes into contact with air, any traces in blood or urine on a toilet seat would die quickly. And even if you touched a doorknob that had some infected fluid on it, you would have to have an open cut on your hand for the virus to get into. This is because the AIDS virus cannot pass through unbroken skin or skin that doesn't have an open cut. Simply shaking hands with someone would not pass along the virus. The only way the virus could possibly be transmitted this way would be if an infected person with an open bleeding sore shook hands with another person who also had an open cut.

So being in casual physical contact with an infected person, the way you might be when playing a contact sport, cannot transmit HIV. However, if a player is injured and is bleeding, it is recommended that you avoid contact with the person's blood.

Some Cautions

Ray, age 14, called the Hot Line because he had a question that a lot of people wonder about. He was never really into dating. But now that he's met someone he really likes, he's got some concerns. "This may sound dumb, but can you get infected from kissing, you know, like French kissing?"

The answer is that researchers have never found cases where HIV was spread by deep kissing or French kissing. Again, the small amounts of the virus that have been found in saliva would not be enough to spread infection. But, because of the potential contact with blood through a mouth sore or cut in the mouth or on the lips, the CDC recommends against engaging in deep kissing with an infected person.

If you know how to give CPR (cardiopulmonary resuscitation) or if you're thinking about taking a class in CPR, you may be wondering about the danger of being in such close contact with another person. (CPR requires breathing air into another person's mouth.) Again, the small amount of the AIDS virus that can be found in saliva would not be enough to transmit AIDS. But lifeguards, police officers, paramedics, and firefighters now wear protective masks when they perform CPR. This is to protect them in case there is any blood that may be infected in the mouth of someone they are resuscitating.

Since the AIDS virus is transmitted through blood, people should avoid sharing razors and toothbrushes. There could be a problem if an infected person cut himself during shaving and then gave the razor to another person to use who also cut himself. By the same token, a person could cut her gums while brushing her teeth and then hand the toothbrush to another person who might also have a mouth sore or cut. The virus could possibly enter the bloodstream under these two circumstances.

Donating Blood

There is absolutely no risk of contracting HIV from donating blood. The needles used to draw blood come in sterile packages, and they are never reused. This is a very important fact to understand, because it is crucial that more people who have noninfected blood donate it for use in medical emergencies.

The Red Cross actually recommends that anyone who has been involved in risky behavior not donate blood. So, if you have any questions about whether or not you would be a good donor candidate, check with your family doctor or other medical professional.

Here's what you should know about how the HIV virus *is* transmitted:

You can get HIV from these fluids when they enter your bloodstream:

■ Infected blood and blood products

■ Infected semen (including the first drop of fluid, even before ejaculation)

■ Infected vaginal fluids

■ Infected breast milk

Blood Transfusions and Transplants

When you need to receive blood because you have been in an accident, you have a serious illness, or you are going to have surgery, it is called a transfusion. HIV can be passed on by a transfusion of an infected person's blood into someone else's body. It can also be transmitted by receiving a transplanted organ or tissue from an infected person.

All blood in the United States is now tested to make sure it is free of the HIV virus. All donated organs and tissue are also tested for HIV. But, unfortunately, before the HIV virus was discovered and a test was developed to screen blood, thousands of people were infected through contaminated blood products. Now that there is a test, blood products are safer. But, there is also a risk involved, because people may donate blood before signs of infection show up on a test. The fear of receiving blood that has been infected has led to something called autologous donation: when someone knows they are going to be hospitalized for surgery, they donate their own blood to be given back to them.

Hemophilia

Hemophilia is a disorder in which an individual's blood does not clot on its own. This condition can cause prolonged, uncontrollable bleeding even from the smallest cut. It can be controlled, though, by frequent infusions of a clotting factor

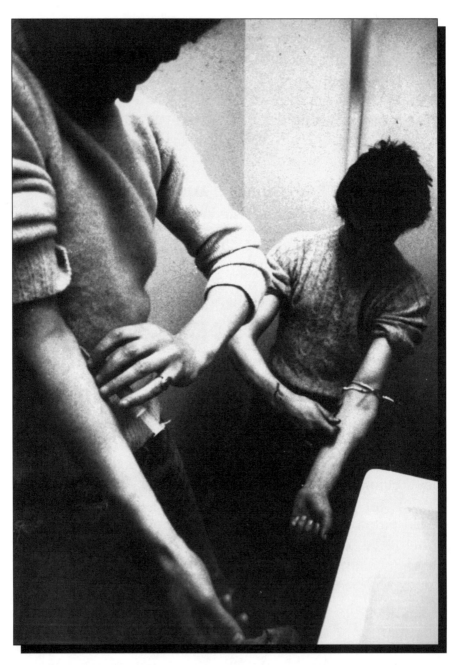

Injecting drugs and sharing needles is extremely risky behavior. Blood from an HIV-infected person can be directly injected from an uncleaned needle into the bloodstream of the next user.

called anti-hemophilic factor (AHF). AHF is a blood product made from pooling thousands of units of blood plasma, which is the clear, liquid part of blood.

Before blood was being tested routinely for HIV, thousands of hemophiliacs became infected with the AIDS virus by receiving contaminated blood. AHF went from being a life-saver to being a potential killer; however, the screening of blood has now made it a safer product.

Intravenous Drug Use

Here's how HIV is spread using needles. When a person uses a needle to inject drugs, it comes into direct contact with that person's blood. When the needle is pulled out, some of the blood is drawn back up into the hollow part of the needle and also into the syringe, the hollow plastic tube that is used to hold the drug being injected. If someone else uses this same needle without cleaning it, the blood from the first person is injected directly into the bloodstream of the second person.

If you know people who inject drugs, first try to convince them to stop. If you can't stop them, try to get them profession-al help. In addition, try to convince them that they *must not* share needles. If they do continue to share needles, then at least they should know the procedures for cleaning them.

Doctors and Dentists

Since doctors and dentists come into contact with blood and body fluids every day, many take precautions by wearing pro-tective gloves. Some may also wear protective goggles or masks to avoid having blood splashed into the eyes or the nose. It is also important that these health professionals prop-erly clean and sterilize any instruments that come in contact with blood or other fluids. Remember, doctors and dentists also want to be sure that they are not infected by their patients.

So, you should feel free to ask questions about what precautions they are taking to protect both of you.

You may have heard also of cases in which doctors, nurses, and other healthcare workers get pricked by a needle and contract the AIDS virus. This can happen, but usually only in cases where large amounts of the virus enter directly into the bloodstream. A few healthcare workers have also been infected by taking care of AIDS patients for a long period of time. But the records show that this has occurred only in cases where the person didn't wear protective gloves when coming in contact with infected bodily fluids.

Sexual Transmission

Having sex and using contaminated needles to inject drugs are the two main ways of spreading the HIV virus. HIV is in the blood, semen (including the first drop of fluid, even before ejaculation), or vaginal secretions of an infected person. HIV can enter the body through the vagina, penis, and rectum, as well as through the mouth, by means of oral sex, especially if sores or cuts are present. Anal sex is especially risky for both men and women.

"Unprotected sex" is sex without the protection of a latex condom. Any form of unprotected sex is unsafe. Although condoms are not perfect, they are highly effective in preventing HIV when used consistently and correctly.

Having sex with multiple partners increases the risk of getting HIV. In a way, your partners' sex partners become *your* partners, and the odds of infection increase sharply.

Infected Babies

Women with HIV can infect their babies. The mother can pass the infection to the baby before it is born or during birth. The baby can also become infected by breastfeeding.

Better Safe Than Sorry

 My brother told me that if you wear a condom during sex, there's no way you can get HIV. Is it really that simple?

 Just as a condom does not offer 100 percent protection from pregnancy, it cannot guarantee that the AIDS virus will not be spread from one partner to another. But right now, next to abstinence—having no sex at all—it is the best protection we have against giving and getting sexually transmitted diseases.

• • • • • • • • • • • •

You've probably heard of the term "safe sex." These days the better term to use is "safer sex," which is what you practice if you use a condom correctly each and every time you have intercourse.

Condoms

If used correctly and continually, condoms can help protect you and your partner from the AIDS virus, as well as from other infections spread by having sex. (They also provide an excellent method of birth control.) A condom is a sheath made of latex or animal skin that fits over the penis when it is erect or hard. It catches a man's semen during ejaculation and therefore prevents the semen from passing into his partner during sex. Only latex condoms should be used, because the animal skin (or natural membrane) condoms contain pores, or holes, and do not provide protection against HIV.

A condom should be used for all kinds of sex, including vaginal, oral, and anal. In order to avoid pregnancy, some teenagers are reported to be having anal intercourse (placing the erect penis in the rectal opening, or anus, of the partner). You should be warned that since this often produces cuts or tears in the fragile tissue of the rectum, without a condom you are not protected against HIV infection.

You can buy condoms at most drugstores or from vending machines. You don't need a prescription or proof of your age to buy one. They are inexpensive and will not cause any serious side effects.

Don't Be Embarrassed

If you are sexually active, don't let embarrassment keep you from getting and using condoms. If you feel you're ready to have sex, then you're ready to think about protecting yourself and your partner. There are some guys who won't wear condoms because they don't think it's "macho," or they think it will interfere with their sexual pleasure. But once you get in the habit of using a condom, it will become natural to you and your partner.

Be Responsible

Some guys also think that just because girls can get pregnant, the girls are solely responsible for using protection. Both partners need to understand that this is something you have to deal with together. This means discussing together prevention of pregnancy and sexually transmitted diseases, and choosing what protection you're going to use.

Trina, a Hot Line caller, is HIV-positive. She started sleeping with her boyfriend when she was 16. She never knew anything about birth control. "I was with this guy who was 21. I figured since he was older, he would take care of it. He told me he

Condoms can help prevent transmission of the HIV virus. They are available in every drugstore at little cost and can be bought without a prescription. Schools in some cities and states provide them without charge. Follow the directions in this book for use.

knew a way to have sex without getting me pregnant and without using birth control, and I believed him. For two years I was bragging to my friends about how I hadn't gotten pregnant. Now that I'm sick with the AIDS virus, I'm certainly not bragging anymore."

How to Use a Condom

It is important to use a condom properly in order for it to be effective. It needs to be put on the penis before any sexual contact. Be sure to put it on correctly. If you don't, there's a possibility that it will slip off, and you will no longer be protected. Here are some simple rules to follow:

■ You should never open the package with your teeth, finger-nails, or other sharp objects. This could put a hole in the condom.

■ Store condoms in a cool, dry place. Never use a condom that has been in your wallet or a glove compartment for a long time. Read the expiration date on the wrapper or on the box the condom came in. If the date has expired, don't use it.

■ Only use latex (rubber) condoms. The ones made from animal skin have small holes in them that can allow the HIV virus to pass through.

■ Don't use condoms that fit only over the head of the penis ("tip condoms"). These can easily leak and offer you no protection against pregnancy or diseases.

■ Use only a water-based lubricant on the condom. (Some condoms come prelubricated.) Put a dot of lubricant inside the tip of the condom and then on the outside. Do not use an oil-based lubricant like petroleum jelly, baby oil, or hand lotion. The oil can cause the condom to break.

To prevent leakage of semen, after ejaculation a man should hold onto the base of the condom firmly as the penis is withdrawn. This needs to be done while the penis is still erect; otherwise, the condom may slip off inside. After a condom has been used, it should be disposed of and never used again.

Spermicides

Though some spermicides kill HIV in test tubes, it is not certain whether they do so in the body during sex. Spermicides should not be used alone to prevent HIV. A spermicide (gel, foam, film, or suppository) may be used *with a condom.* Follow the directions on the package: the spermicide should be put directly into the body. Spermicide-lubricated condoms do not contain enough spermicide to prevent HIV transmission.

It does not help to add spermicide inside the condom. If the condom should break, infected semen could pass into the body before the spermicide could spread out. And because some spermicides cause irritations and sores, these may allow any HIV in the semen to enter the body.

To find out if you are allergic to a spermicide, rub a little on the inside of your wrist and look for a reaction on the skin. If you have a reaction, don't use the spermicide. You can actually increase the risk of HIV transmission if an allergic reaction occurs.

Risky Business

There are all kinds of risky behavior that you know you should avoid, like taking drugs, drinking alcohol, and using weapons or firearms. You also know that unprotected sex can lead to pregnancy. Because of the AIDS virus, unprotected sex can also lead to illness and eventually death. The only way to be sure that you will not get HIV from sex is to practice abstinence— no sex at all. This may not be easy, depending on your circumstances, but you have to think about the consequences. This is the time to take control of your life.

The Domino Theory

If abstinence doesn't work for you, and you are going to be sexually active, you must take further precautions to limit the number of sexual partners you have. You can also never be absolutely sure about your partner's past, so start with the assumption that your partner is HIV positive (even if this is very unlikely), and be sure to take precautions. You probably never thought of it this way, but every time you have sex with someone, in a sense you're having sex with all the people they have slept with before. It's sort of like the domino theory—when you set up rows and rows of dominoes and you knock down the first one, which in turn knocks down the next one and the next one, creating a chain reaction and causing all the dominoes to be knocked down. If the dominoes were people, and the first person was infected with the AIDS virus, he or she could pass it on to the next person, who could give it to the next person, and so on.

How It Works

Here's another way to explain it. Ruth has never been sexually involved with anyone before. She meets Robert, who seems like a great guy. He's good-looking, athletic, and a lot of fun to be with. Robert asks Ruth to go out with him, and she does. After a few months go by, Robert wants to have sex with Ruth. Ruth loves and trusts Robert and thinks she's ready for this next step. But what Robert never told Ruth is that before they met, he used to go out with Rochelle. Robert broke up with Rochelle because he found out she was sleeping with Dan at the same time that she was seeing him. Dan was on the school wrestling team, and he was really hung up about his size and strength. He and a friend, Will, started taking steroids intravenously. Dan and Will were sharing needles, and Dan became infected with the HIV virus.

When Dan found out he was infected, he told Rochelle. But do you think Rochelle told Robert? It's not very likely, since Rochelle didn't want Robert to know about Dan. So, when Ruth had sex with Robert, from an infection standpoint it was as if she were having sex with Rochelle, Dan, and Will, as well. Because Robert seemed like a nice, healthy guy, Ruth never thought about the risks she was taking. If she had, she would have thought twice about becoming sexually involved with him.

The point is, you can never be 100 percent sure. But it's better to be safe than to be sorry.

Reducing Risk

■ Remember that abstinence is the only sure means of protecting yourself against AIDS.

■ If you are sexually active, use a latex condom every time you have intercourse.

■ Limit your sexual partners.

■ Find out all you can about your sexual partner.

Openly discussing pregnancy and HIV risks with your partner is not as difficult as it may seem.

■ Avoid using alcohol or drugs.

■ Avoid using intravenous drugs and sharing needles.

It Couldn't Happen to Me

You've probably heard people say, "You can't get AIDS just from sleeping with one person." Wrong! It just takes one time with an infected person to change your life forever.

Alison Gertz's Story

Alison Gertz, a 26-year-old woman who died of AIDS in 1992, found that out the hard way. She was able to track the exact time when she got infected with the AIDS virus from a "one-night stand" she had with a bartender she had met in New York City. She was 16 at the time. She and her friends used to frequent the bar and club scene. Although the guy showed up at Alison's door with champagne and roses, their night together was not exactly a dream date. The bartender was so high on cocaine that he wasn't even able to ejaculate. Even so, enough infected fluid was able to enter her body to transmit the AIDS virus. Six years after the incident, she came down with pneumonia and learned that she was HIV-positive. She also discovered that the bartender had died of AIDS in 1986.

Alison later suffered from mycobacterial infection (MAI), an AIDS-related illness (see p. 51). It was so awful that some nights she had to take morphine to kill the pain. At one point she was suicidal. But eventually she was able to reach a state of calm. She found strength in publicizing her story in order to help others. She allowed a TV movie to be made about her life, called *Something to Live For.* She spoke out on TV and lectured at colleges, warning that *anyone* has a risk of getting the disease. She was living proof of that. Alison was an unlikely person to get AIDS. She had never had a blood transfusion, she didn't use IV drugs, and she hadn't had many different sexual partners. But in the end, it all came down to that one night.

It's easy to think that you're immortal—that you'll live forever—and to believe that nothing bad could ever happen to you. But to keep yourself and other people you care about safe, it's important not to take chances that you might regret later.

Getting Tested

If you have any reason to think you might have been infected with HIV, you may want to consider being tested. Anyone, at any age, can be tested for HIV, and it's not necessary to tell anyone or to get permission from an adult. There are many free, anonymous testing centers around the country. To find one near you, call one of the numbers in the back of this book, or call your doctor, Planned Parenthood, or a pregnancy counseling center.

When you take the test, you may be given a number or a code. So instead of using your name or Social Security number, you will be identified by your code. This way you will be anonymous, and no one will ever be able to associate you with your test results.

Some private doctors and clinics do not do anonymous testing, but they promise that the test results will be kept confidential. However, you cannot be 100 percent sure that the records will stay confidential. Abuse is common. Your results may be made part of your insurance, hospital, medical, financial, or employment records. However, many states have made laws placing limits on disclosing confidential HIV information and requiring the consent of the person tested.

Since a test for HIV became available in 1985, there have been concerns about the use of information to discriminate against persons with HIV. Testing in the United States has been mainly voluntary. However, tests are required for induction into the military and for certain federal jobs, for immigration into the United States, and by some insurance companies who don't want to insure people with HIV.

Take Someone with You

Deciding to go and then actually going for the test may take courage. There is no reason you must go alone, however. Take someone with you. The obvious companion is your sex partner, who may also want to be tested. If your partner won't go, confide in a good friend, and ask him or her to go with you.

Teresa, age 16, was afraid to get tested. She wasn't sure she wanted to know if she had the virus or not. But when she thought about the possible consequences, she finally made the decision to go ahead. "I asked my friend to go with me, so I wouldn't have to be alone. That made a big difference. She went back with me when it was time to get my results. They were negative, and we *both* wept with relief."

Don't Put It Off

Although you're scared, and it's a difficult step to take, don't put off being tested. There are three main reasons why it's important to get tested early. First, if you test positive, you can learn better health habits and start taking medications that could help you stay healthy longer. Second, again if you test positive, you'll need to contact the people with whom you've engaged in risky behavior. If you feel this is too difficult for you to do yourself, some agencies will contact these people for you. Third, if the test results are negative and you have been engaging in risky behavior, be grateful that you have been given a second chance to begin acting responsibly. Do not take it as a sign that you are immune to getting the virus. If you have been taking precautions, continue doing so—don't let down your guard.

The HIV Test

When the body encounters a germ or virus like HIV, the immune system tries to fight back by producing antibodies to attack it. The HIV tests search the blood for these antibodies. The simplest test is called the ELISA test (enzyme-linked immunosorbent assay). Sometimes the test indicates the presence of HIV antibodies in blood samples when they actually do not exist, producing a so-called false-positive result. Because this can happen, every positive reading from an antibody test is checked again with a further, more specific and more time-consuming test, called the Western blot. If the Western blot test is positive, then the positive reading is confirmed.

If an ELISA test results in a negative reading, it can mean two things: one, you are not infected; or, two, the presence of the HIV antibodies has not yet shown up in your body. It can take up to six months for the immune system to develop antibodies. If you are tested very soon after contracting the virus, you will not yet have produced enough antibodies in your blood system for the test to identify. For this reason, if you have been involved in risky behavior, you need to be tested again in six months.

CHAPTER 4

It's Just Not Fair

Q Freddie, this little eight-year-old kid on my street, has AIDS. Turns out his mother was an IV drug user. Now everyone treats him like he's got the plague. There are even parents in his school who want to have him kicked out. It's just not fair. He's just a little kid. It's not his fault that he got sick. Why do people blame him for it? What can I do to make life easier for him?

A Sounds like you're already on the right track. You definitely should take his side and understand that what he needs is support, not blame. Maybe you can start having some friendly talks with him and his mother. That will support them and set a good example for other people to follow.

• • • • • • • • • • • •

Blaming people for having AIDS comes from fear and lack of knowledge. AIDS has turned into an epidemic, and people are afraid of catching it, like any infectious disease. They don't know the facts about how HIV is spread, and think they should avoid anybody who has it. Furthermore, the disease is associated with taking drugs and having sex, activities that often imply something negative in our culture. Therefore, if you get AIDS, you must have done something wrong and deserve it.

Aside from finding a cure, the only hope now for preventing the further spread of AIDS is widespread public education that results in a change in the way people behave. Blaming individuals, or groups of individuals, for having the disease solves nothing.

The Case of Ryan White

There have been cases in which children have been barred from their schools because they had AIDS. Perhaps the best-known case involved Ryan White. Ryan was a hemophiliac from Kokomo, Indiana. He received a tainted batch of factor VIII, a blood product given to hemophiliacs. He was diagnosed in December 1984, when he was 13. AIDS was so new that no one was sure how it was transmitted. The announcement of the discovery of the AIDS virus had only been made in April of that same year. Even the Centers for Disease Control (CDC) had not published its guidelines on dealing with AIDS.

The public school system began the process of trying to keep him out of school. Ryan and his mother fought a long legal battle over the issues of the case. They suffered hostility, insults, and name-calling from other people in the community.

Certain Conditions
Finally, the decision was made to allow Ryan to attend school under certain conditions. He would have to use separate eating utensils and a separate bathroom, and he could not drink from the hall water fountains. He would not be allowed to go to the gym or to swim in the pool. The building would also have to be disinfected every night.

Almost half the students were kept home as a sign of protest by their parents. People also picketed outside of the school building. After a bullet was fired through their living room window, the Whites moved to another town.

By then, Ryan had become a national figure, and he received a lot of public support from well-known people. Olympic diving champion Greg Louganis gave him his winning medal;

Ryan White, age 14, returns to school in Kokomo, Indiana, in June, 1986, followed by reporters. A court dissolved a temporary restraining order keeping Ryan, who had AIDS, from attending school. Before he died in 1990, Ryan had become nationally known for his fight for AIDS awareness.

Elton John flew him to Disneyland; and he was a guest on Johnny Carson's "Tonight" show on TV. In schools and other places, he made many public appearances to speak out about AIDS, including one appearance before the Presidential Commission on AIDS. Ryan died in 1990 at age 18. He is memorialized on the AIDS quilt as "Educator for Life."

Babies with AIDS

On average, about 25 percent of pregnant women infected with HIV pass along the virus to their babies, either before or during birth. HIV can also be passed along through breastfeeding. In the United States, doctors recommend that an infected mother give her baby formula instead of breast milk.

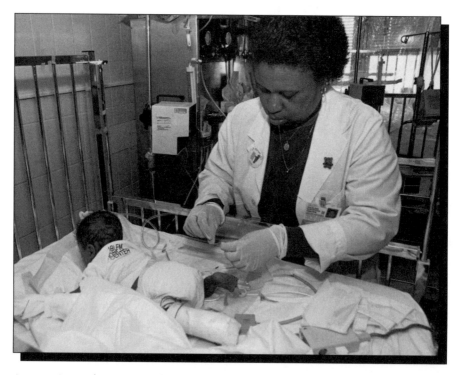

A nurse in Harlem Hospital in New York City takes a blood sample from a baby with AIDS. The staff at the hospital stresses loving care for the children.

All babies from infected mothers test HIV-positive at birth. A year and a half or more later, when a baby develops its own immune system, the baby may test negative. It is estimated that by 1994, 7,500 children in the United States will have developed AIDS. Many are abandoned by a parent too sick to care for the child. Most will end up as orphans when both parents are infected and die. It is believed that during the next decade at least 125,000 children will become orphans due to deaths from AIDS.

Hale House

City hospitals are crowded with AIDS babies. These babies are no different from any other baby. They need to be held, cared

Mother Clara Hale, noted for her work with drug, alcohol, and AIDS infected children, celebrates her 83rd birthday with some of the children at Hale House in New York City.

for, and loved. Some people even volunteer at hospitals simply to hold AIDS babies. In New York City, Hale House was started by Clara Hale and her daughter, Dr. Lorraine Hale. The home was established to care for children abandoned by drug-addicted and alcoholic parents. But now many of the children at Hale House have AIDS or have been abandoned by parents with AIDS. Homes are sought for these children, but many people fear the disease and don't want to have these children in their homes. Other people may not be concerned about infection because they know how HIV is transmitted, but they may resist taking a child with AIDS because they are reluctant about getting attached to a child with a fatal disease. Thus, these children face a very uncertain future.

Getting Involved

When André, age 14, found out that his older brother Victor had AIDS, he was devastated. "We have always been so close, and now I don't know how to act toward him."

Fortunately, André's family was sensitive and supportive in the situation. Though it was a very emotional time for them all, family members sat down and talked together, found out all they could about the disease, and spoke with an AIDS counselor. Because Victor was not willing to tell his friends or other people yet, the family decided they would keep the disease a secret for the time being. Victor needed some time to come to terms with his feelings. On his part, André was able to be there for his brother. He talked things over with Victor, encouraged him, and made a real difference in his life.

Other Things You Can Do
Finding out that someone close to you is HIV-positive or has AIDS is upsetting emotionally. You may not know how to approach the person. One way to figure out how that person might want to be treated is to put yourself in his or her shoes.

Try asking yourself these questions:

- What if it were me?

- Do I want to tell my family? How will they react?

- Will my friends abandon me? Will they be afraid of me?

- Is there any hope for the future for me?

The best way you can treat someone else is the same way you would want to be treated if you were in his or her place.

Once you have offered your support to someone, remember a few guidelines:

- Be a good listener.

- Respect people's privacy by not discussing their illness with anybody else without their permission.

- Find out about support groups both for persons with HIV or AIDS and for their relatives or friends.

- Continue to find out all you can about the disease.

Making a Difference

If you understand the disease and can help others understand it, it will make an enormous difference. People working together can help change behaviors that spread HIV. If you learn how to prevent the spread of infection, you can teach others. You can pass along information and perhaps change people's negative attitudes.

What Can You Do?
Make sure your school and community libraries have pamphlets and books about AIDS. Suggest to your local librarian,

teacher, or the principal of your school that it would be important to have a speaker come to educate others about the disease.

Join an AIDS awareness group or form your own. Be a volunteer at a local AIDS organization, offer to answer phones at a teen hot line, or be a peer counselor to people your own age. You can also volunteer to be a buddy to someone with AIDS. This means you might do errands, shop, bring meals, read aloud, or just keep him or her company. You and your friends can make a difference.

Survey Response to Treatment of People with HIV/AIDS **(Percentage of people surveyed who agreed with statements)**		
	1987	1991
People with AIDS should be treated with compassion	78%	91%
An employee with AIDS should be liable for dismissal by an employer	33%	21%
A tenant with AIDS should be liable for eviction by the landlord	17%	10%
Would refuse to work alongside someone with AIDS	25%	16%
Anyone who tests positive for HIV antibodies should have to carry an identification card	60%	59%
A person with AIDS should be isolated from society	21%	10%

Source: Adapted from "Large Majorities Continue to Back AIDS Testing," by George Gallup, Jr., and Dr. Frank Newport, in *The Gallup Poll Monthly*, May 1991.

CHAPTER 5

Living with AIDS

Q I see people who are HIV-positive, like Magic Johnson, walking around like there's nothing wrong with them. Maybe AIDS doesn't affect everyone in the same way. And maybe, if you just take good care of yourself, you can be cured of AIDS, right?

A There are several different stages that the human body goes through once it is infected with HIV. People may remain healthy for years, especially if they take care of themselves. But, so far, there is no cure for the disease. People infected with HIV will eventually die of an AIDS-related illness.

· · · · · · · · · · · ·

How AIDS Progresses

Here's how AIDS develops from the time of infection from the HIV virus.

The Asymptomatic Period
Two to twelve weeks after infection the body begins to produce antibodies, which can then be detected in an antibody test. For months or even years, a person with the virus may have no symptoms and be totally free from infection. Many will not even know they are HIV-positive unless they have gone for the anti-body test. (Some people experience swollen lymph nodes, a rash, a fever, a sore throat, and fatigue soon after being infected.)

The announcement in 1991 that basketball star "Magic" Johnson is infected with HIV has helped to awaken all Americans to the threat of AIDS.

There are many reasons why this period varies so much with different people. Having good nutrition, enough exercise, enough rest, and a general sense of well-being all contribute to prolonging this asymptomatic period. A person who gets immunizations and avoids exposure to infections will probably stay well longer. People who abuse their bodies by doing drugs or drinking may get sicker more quickly. These activities are damaging to the immune system.

Another factor includes the amount of virus present in the bloodstream and the number of strains of the virus a person has. The smaller the amount and the fewer the strains of virus someone has, the slower the infection will proceed. If a person has more than one strain, there is a greater chance of getting sick faster.

Lastly, the person's genetic history is a factor. There are some people who simply cannot fight off infection as quickly or as well as others. Even though a person may be asymptomatic, he or she can lose T-cells. Most people lose a high percentage of their T-cells before full-blown AIDS develops. Depending on the person, the amount of T-cells and the pace at which they are destroyed will vary.

Development of Symptoms
The early stage of AIDS was once called ARC (AIDS Related Complex). Today someone in this stage is said to be "symptomatic" or to "have HIV disease." The problems for people in this stage can range from mild to severe. They may suffer from many of the same symptoms as those with AIDS, but they don't yet have one of the illnesses or the low T-cell count that defines AIDS. Symptoms can include chills, fever, night sweats, diarrhea, rashes, weight loss, fatigue, a dry cough, and persistently swollen lymph nodes.

Full-blown AIDS
Renée, age 19, watched her friend Laura die of AIDS. "Laura and I had been friends since we were little kids. When she told me she had AIDS, I thought it was a bad joke. I said to her, 'Only guys get AIDS.' Now that she's gone, I know it was no joke. Laura was sick all the time. Sometimes it was hard to believe that she was the same age as me. She was tired all the time, and it was like she had a cold 24 hours a day, every day.

It really hurt to see her that way. I never thought I'd lose my best friend forever like that. She was only 19."

AIDS is the last stage of the HIV disease and begins when a person contracts one of the opportunistic infections. The CDC definition of AIDS includes anyone who is HIV-positive and has a T-cell count of 200 or below. Doctors recommend preventive and antiviral treatment for anyone with a T-cell count below 200. Under normal healthy conditions, opportunistic infections can be fought off. But for a person with a suppressed immune system, this is difficult. Studies show that most people who die of AIDS-related causes have T-cell counts under 50, when the immune system has basically stopped functioning.

The Diseases of AIDS

AIDS Dementia Complex (ADC)

Many people infected with AIDS suffer from AIDS dementia complex. The most likely cause of this is HIV affecting the brain directly. There can be many degrees of dementia. In all cases it causes a person's mind to become cloudy; it takes longer for the person to organize thoughts and to remember things. Physically, a person may become unsteady and uncoordinated. In the worst cases, there may be personality change, difficulty in speaking and concentrating, and psychosis, or severe mental disorder. Neurological symptoms, including ordinary depression, are also associated with other opportunistic infections, so that numerous tests are often necessary to diagnose ADC.

Kaposi's Sarcoma (KS)

This disease appears as purple or black lesions or wounds on the skin. It was originally thought to be a skin cancer, but doctors no longer think of it as a true cancer. Instead, they believe it may be another virus that is sexually transmitted. KS can appear when the T-cell count is still relatively high (between

200 and 800), so infected people can live with it for a long time. The lesions can grow at variable speeds and can be in remission, or stop growing, for periods of time.

Lymphoma
Lymphoma (cancer of the lymph system) is becoming increasingly common among people with AIDS. Lymphoma is life-threatening. Symptoms include painless enlargement of the nodes, fever, night sweats, and weight loss. If the disease is in the central nervous system, it can cause headaches, confusion, memory loss, weakness, and seizures. No method of prevention is known, and all treatment is experimental at present.

Mycobacterium Avium Intracellulare (MAI)
MAI is caused by common bacteria related to the organism that causes tuberculosis. It commonly causes high fever, night sweats, weakness, diarrhea, and stomach pain. MAI is found particularly in people with AIDS who live for several years following their diagnosis. MAI rarely develops unless the T-cell count is lower than 50.

Pneumocystis carinii pneumonia (PCP)
Formerly a rare type of pneumonia, PCP is the most common opportunistic illness among people with AIDS. It is an infection of the lungs that usually causes a dry cough, fever, and shortness of breath. These symptoms deserve immediate attention because PCP can develop rapidly in a person with a T-cell count below 200. PCP is responsible for more deaths than any other AIDS-related illness. When caught early, however, PCP is entirely treatable.

Toxoplasmosis
This serious brain infection may cause headaches, fever, seizures, and neurological problems; severe cases may cause blindness and coma. It is acquired by eating raw meat or by

contact with the feces of infected cats. People with T-cell counts below 200 should take preventive treatment.

Tuberculosis (TB)
People with HIV are at special risk for infection with the germ that causes tuberculosis. Skin tests are recommended for all HIV-positive people, and preventive treatment has become standard.

Medical Treatments

Researchers have discovered treatments that try to prevent the AIDS virus from reproducing itself in the body. Three drugs that are currently approved by the FDA (Food and Drug Administration) are AZT, ddI, and ddC. However, none of these antivirals permanently rids the body of HIV, and some of them are toxic (poisonous) and cause severe side effects. They are also very expensive. The cost of AZT per person has been estimated at $10,000 annually.

Another antiviral called d4T is currently in clinical trials. Clinical trials are tests of drugs that have shown promise but have not yet proven effective. The trials suggest that d4T improves patients' conditions, and it has been found to increase T-cell counts in most patients tested. In order for patients to qualify for trials, they must have a T-cell count under 300, be unable to tolerate AZT or ddI, or have deteriorating health problems even after treatment with AZT or ddI.

Recent Findings
Longer-term studies now report that the effect of AZT and other drugs often wears off after a year or two and does not always guarantee longer life. There is also some question as to whether people should use AZT at the beginning of their illness, while they are still healthy, or take it once they have begun to suffer from the opportunistic infections that severely attack the immune system. Also, it has been known for some

time that the antivirals cause harmful side effects to the system (for example, sleep problems, leg cramps, headaches, nausea, diarrhea, or anemia).

On the other side of the argument, while there are many problems with the antiviral drugs and treatments, some patients are living healthier lives because of them. Some have extended their lives for extra months or even years. Antiviral drugs also can boost T-cell counts and benefit people with neurological complications or dementia. Taking a combination of antivirals often works more successfully than taking one by itself.

In Search of a Vaccine
The eventual goal for treating HIV is to have a vaccine for people to take the way they do now for diseases like polio, measles, smallpox, and mumps. Many researchers are current-

Though no cure has yet been found for AIDS, researchers are constantly developing new antivirals and other drugs that show benefit to patients in clinical trials.

ly working to develop one. One reason why it has been so diffi-cult is because HIV is a *retrovirus*. A retrovirus is able to become part of the genetic material of the cell it attacks and infects. So when the cell reproduces itself, it produces more HIV. Another reason is because the virus acts differently in dif-ferent people. Because there is still much to learn about HIV and AIDS, it is uncertain how long it will take to find a vaccine that will make HIV a manageable disorder.

Alternative Medicine

Many people who are infected with HIV have no access to tra-ditional medicines, can't pay for them, or find they don't work. Others regard AZT as toxic and refuse to take it. They often are searching for alternatives and believe in the benefit from them. It is an individual choice. While some people may find certain benefits from such alternative treatments, they should remem-ber that there is still no known cure for the disease.

■ *Underground drugs* include any drugs that are not approved by the FDA. This means they have not gone through official testing procedures. Some come from other countries and are passed on to people through AIDS activist groups, who believe that U.S. research is not progressing fast enough.

■ Some people believe that *a change in diet* can alter the effects of HIV. Many try a macrobiotic diet that consists mainly of vegetables and grains.

■ There are many *vitamins and food supplements* that are said to slow down the growth of HIV or help the immune system. Some of these are garlic, vitamin C, vitamin A, zinc, and AL721, a substance that comes from egg yolk.

■ There are several other alternative treatments for AIDS.

Chiropractic treatment is based on the alignment of a person's backbone. *Acupuncture* is part of the Chinese culture. The treatment involves inserting needles in any of 365 different points along twelve body lines. The needles are left in place for twenty to thirty minutes over a period of several days or months. Another Chinese practice is to use *herbal medicines* in various combinations.

Positive Strategies

Exercise can certainly be beneficial to persons infected with the virus, because it can make them feel better and stronger. They might try traditional workout programs, weight lifting, or yoga (a Hindu system of balancing the mind and the body through breathing and posturing exercises).

You may have heard the saying "Laughter is the best medicine." In fact, doctors say that people who can laugh can cope better with serious illness. Some people searching for an alternative believe that working on their mental health and having control of their illness can help keep them physically healthy.

The Will to Live

AIDS is a complicated disease. It has a physical side, which deals with the various illnesses that the human body must endure, and it also has a psychological side. AIDS involves a whole range of emotional problems. An infected person may feel sad, hopeless, angry, scared, anxious, depressed, guilty, ashamed, nervous, and irritable. At first, persons diagnosed with HIV may be confused about what their diagnosis means; they may have questions about how AIDS is transmitted; they may wonder how long they have to live and what the quality of their life will be like. Next, they will have to deal with illnesses and being dependent on others. And finally, they will have to face the reality of their own death.

People react in different ways to what's happening to them. Some people deny they're infected and go on engaging in risky behavior. Others feel a sense of low self-esteem. They become obsessed with their health and are afraid to be around other people for fear of infecting them. Some give up and turn to drugs and alcohol; they avoid getting proper medical care and even contemplate suicide.

On the other hand, some people have turned their lives around upon learning they were infected with HIV: they have given up drugs, for example, and put their lives back together. Others have been HIV-positive for as long as 17 years and are still healthy.

People with AIDS need to fight their feelings of powerlessness and isolation. The best way to achieve this is by channeling their energy into a positive direction. They might educate themselves about the disease, become educated health care consumers, get involved in AIDS organizations, help others, explore new treatments, eat a healthy diet, reduce stress, and think positively. The will to live can be very powerful.

Joseph Luis Lopez, Jr., who was HIV-positive from birth, died of AIDS at age 15 in 1994. Joe spent three summers at a camp called the Hole in the Wall Gang Camp for children with life-threatening diseases. He collaborated on a book with six other campers and two counselors. The book is called *I Will Sing Life: Voices from the Hole in the Wall*. In the book, Joe says:

> HIV is nothing. It's just a virus. It's just like being sick for a long time, for always. I say, put on your gloves and fight 'em, go 10 rounds. You have to beat it. But some people, they're scared, they just say, "Nah, I can't beat it, I can't." They don't care about themselves because they think they're dying. I got nothing to talk about dying. I ain't dying yet.

Interview

Karen is a social worker who works in a home for adolescent girls with AIDS and their children. The girls live in a large, modest but pleasantly furnished older house in a run-down area not far from the center of a city. They each have their own room and share laundry and kitchen facilities. A fenced area in the rear contains play equipment for the children.

We'll be three years old this June. We're a group house for adolescent women who are HIV-positive. We also take girls who are pregnant, and those who already have children can stay together here.

The girls are referred to us from various sources; for example, some are referred by the Department of Social Services. We've also gotten some referrals from hospitals. We'll take them from anywhere. We have an outreach worker who found one girl on the street. He goes out and talks in the schools and meets people in the community, and he heard about this girl who was homeless. She was living in an abandoned building with her baby. So he helped bring her here.

This is a private facility, but we receive funding from the state if the state places a child here through a social worker. We also receive some funding from the Department of Health. But we have people who are not placed by the state, and we'll work with that. Like, we have a young woman here who is on welfare, and she gives us $100 a month in rent. We also get some donations. But the state pays $152 a day, because these kids are qualified legally as "medically fragile." So having the state-placed kids here can subsidize some other people.

All the girls have to be involved in some sort of educational program. Several of them are getting their GED [General Equivalency Diploma]. Two of our girls do have their high school diplomas, and they're going to a local community college. That's a big focus. If they have children, we expect them to take care of their children. We have staff support to help instruct them, but they're really responsible for the feeding, the bathing, and the children's medical appointments.

All the women are HIV-positive—that's what got them in the program. Newborns with HIV-positive mothers will automatically test positive because they have the mothers' antibodies. Then there's a window period of about 18 months to 3 years when they can convert to negative once they have their own immune systems. And we actually have one child here who did that. Another child here is 18 months old and is remaining positive. We have another child who is 8 months old, and the test is still borderline. So, there's a lot of waiting involved.

A lot of our girls are really surprised when they find out they are HIV-positive, because they don't think it could happen to them. We have one girl here who was 19 when she contracted HIV. She said she couldn't believe it—she had only had three partners when she found out. And she said she didn't think any of them would have the virus or pass it on.

They all show different levels of accepting it. Some of the kids can talk about it, about their fears and concerns about dying. Some of the girls leave the room, though, if the subject is brought up. Of course, some of the girls haven't known for all that long—a couple have known for only a few months. It takes time to accept what's happening to them. They have the virus, and there's no cure. They're going to have it forever, and it's a scary thing.

People are still hiding the disease. If they don't have a place like this to come to, if they're lucky they'll have a family who will support them. But we have a young woman here who was 18 years old when she came, and she has never told her mother that she has the virus. She knew there was a chance that her family members would turn their backs. Certainly some of the girls' families have turned their backs. Doesn't matter who they are: black, white, or Hispanic, if their families have turned their backs, they don't have much left.

There still seems to be a lot of shame attached to the disease. People still want to know how you got it—like you're a bad person, you must have done something wrong. You had sex or were using drugs, so you deserve to get it. These are just kids who never really understood the full ramifications of what they were doing, and no one deserves ending up like that.

One of our girls who grew up in a very abusive home was molested by her father, became pregnant by him at age 12 or 13, and had an abortion. Then at 14 she had a baby by her boyfriend. She's not really sure who she got the virus from. Another of our girls became pregnant and infected after being raped. There are stories like that.

All of the girls are at different levels of the disease. There are one or two who could be classified as having AIDS. But from their appearances, you wouldn't know they were HIV-positive. I think what we're doing here is providing stability—a clean house, a well-balanced diet, and helping them take their medication regularly.

The mothers feel really guilty about their children, like the one 18-month-old we have here who is testing positive. She was delayed, and she's not walking yet. And the mother was the one who was pregnant because of rape. It's really hard for her to see her baby struggling. Her baby was very sick when she was born; for a while we didn't think she was going to make it. She's doing really well now, but it's been tough for the mother.

When I go out and talk to people, at a party maybe, and mention where I work, usually the next question down the line is, how did the kids get the virus? You don't ask somebody who had a heart attack, how come you got the heart attack? Don't you know about high cholesterol—about cutting down on all those fatty things you eat? You don't think that, but with HIV there still seems to be that next question—how did you get the virus? Like, what did you do that was wrong?

It shouldn't matter why you got the disease. It's spreading, and the scary thing is that it's spreading among children, among adolescents. Maybe they use condoms *once in a while*. Our girl Rita, who got the virus from her boyfriend, said she was using condoms *most of the time.* She didn't realize that that's not good enough, and now she has the virus. It didn't seem real to her. I'd like to make it real to kids. It's *really* out there.

The women here not only have to think about themselves but also about their children. If they already have children, they may have passed the virus on—one mother here has. And if a girl hasn't had a child yet, she realizes she never will have one, or never should have one, because it's bad for her health.

It's a lot of work just to keep up with the new studies that come out. A couple of weeks ago, I read in a magazine about a study that didn't sound very hopeful. It was about taking AZT over the long term—whether it made any difference if people took it or not. That's scary, too. All these kids are on AZT, but you're not really sure if it's going to be helpful to them in the long term.

They can stay here till the end. For a lot of these kids, we are their family—their own families have turned their backs on them. And we don't want to be turning away from them at the time when they need support the most.

I want kids to know how serious this is and to really think about their actions. What they do now could bring them a terminal illness! And also, if they know people—friends or family members—who have the virus, they need to understand that these people need help, they need someone to be there for them. They need their family and their friends. I just want kids to stop and think.

CHAPTER 6

Learning to Cope

Q A good friend of my mother's—of the whole family— was dying of AIDS. I was afraid to go see him at first. I never had anyone close to me die before. I finally did go. It was the hardest thing I ever had to do. Now that he's gone, it hurts so much. I know it sounds really stupid, but I wish people didn't have to die. Will I ever get used to his death?

A We go through many stages when we're grieving for someone who has died. In the beginning, it feels like we'll never get over it. But after awhile, we find it does get easier. The important thing is to move ahead with our own lives. This doesn't mean that we should forget the person who has died. But it does mean that we can't let death take over our life.

• • • • • • • • • • • •

It is difficult to make sense out of any death, but it is especially hard when a young person dies. Watching someone die of AIDS can be very painful. It means seeing a healthy person deteriorate into someone you don't even recognize anymore.

Feelings About Death

Anger
Anger is a normal, healthy emotion. It's natural to feel angry after someone dies, to question why this had to happen. When

someone dies of AIDS, you may find yourself blaming the person for getting sick. But this doesn't mean you love him or her any less. You may be angry at the doctors and other caregivers for not doing enough. You may be angry at the government for ignoring AIDS for so long and for not providing enough money for AIDS research. You may be angry at the people who are prejudiced against those with AIDS or against their friends and relatives. You may be angry at yourself for having been unable to take control of the situation. You need to know how to release this anger in a healthy, safe way and channel it in a more positive direction.

Guilt

After any death, you may also feel guilty that you didn't spend enough time with the person, that you didn't do all you could for him or her. Sometimes people suffering from AIDS can be very difficult to be around. They're feeling all the same emotions you're feeling, but on top of that they are seriously ill. While they were sick, you may have had to wait on them hand and foot. You may have complained about it to them or to other people. Now that they're gone, this can make you feel guilty as well.

Some people have AIDS and keep it a secret. They may want to spare the feelings of the people they love and guard them from having to care for someone who is dying. They may be afraid of how they will be judged. They may feel others will pity them and treat them as victims. They may not be able to bear the pain their death may cause for the people they love. Or, they may be afraid their friends and family will desert them. You and your friends and relatives may feel guilty that you didn't pick up on the signs, that you weren't more sensitive to the situation. You think to yourselves, "If I had only known, I could have been there for him or her." You can't help wondering if the person who died thought that you were purposely staying away.

Depression

The great loss you feel after a death may make you feel severely depressed. Take the time you need to grieve. You may find it hurts to think about the person who is gone. Things may happen that make you think of times you shared together. You may enjoy having these memories, or they may be upsetting to you. You have to figure out the best way for you to handle your emotions. If thinking about the person who died makes you feel bad, then try pushing these thoughts in the background until it's easier for you emotionally.

If you find that you're being overwhelmed by depression, you need to get help. Talk to a parent or a counselor. Find out if your school has a psychologist or social worker on staff. The information at the back of the book can be of help to you.

Carl, age 16, watched his sister die of AIDS. "I was so angry at her, at myself, at the world. My mother kept trying to get me to talk to someone, but I thought it was a big waste of time. My sister was dead, what was talking going to do? I started screwing up at school—getting into trouble a lot. It got so bad, I didn't care if I lived or died. But one day I saw my Mom sitting on my sister's bed, crying. I thought about how she must feel. She had already lost one of her children. What if she lost another? I talked to her about getting help, and she made an appointment for us to speak to a family therapist."

It's important that you don't hold back your feelings. When you get to the point where you can deal with your loss, thinking of this person will no longer be as painful.

Arthur Ashe's Story

Arthur Ashe was a professional tennis player who won some of the greatest championships in the game, including Wimbledon, the U.S. Open, and the World Cup Tennis Finals. He was also the captain of the U.S. Davis Cup Team and was the first African American person to break the color bar in international tennis. He was as respected for his efforts to end racism as he was for his sports ability.

In 1992, after a newspaper threatened to announce it first, he was forced to come forward and tell the American public that he had AIDS. It was a matter that he had wanted to keep private. But the newspaper decided that because Arthur Ashe was a public figure, it was everyone's business to know. As Ashe said in his press conference, "I didn't commit any crime, and I'm not running for public office. I should be able to reserve the right to keep things like that private."

Here are the facts. In 1979, Arthur Ashe suffered a heart attack. He had to have two different bypass operations. During the second, he was given a blood transfusion from a contaminated blood supply. This was in 1983, two years before blood banks began to screen for HIV. He found out that he was HIV-positive five years later when he was again in the hospital, this time for brain surgery.

A Family Copes
Ashe and his wife, Jeanne, also had to tell their five-year-old daughter, Camera, about his illness. She understood that her father was ill, and that he needed to be loved and cared for, just as she did when she was not well. Having explained AIDS to Camera, Arthur and Jeanne realized that it was also important to be able to explain it to Camera's friends and to other children.

Jeanne decided to write a book for families in order to share the Ashes' experience with them and to help them discuss AIDS with their children. The book presents Camera as the speaker and is illustrated with photographs of Camera and Arthur. It was published in 1993 under the title *Daddy and Me*.

The book chronicles the good days as well as the bad. It shows how important it is for families to be supportive of a loved one who is suffering from AIDS. It also communicates that a loving relationship with casual physical contact is safe

In April, 1992, tennis champion Arthur Ashe, with his wife, Jeanne, announced to the world that he had AIDS. Together they spoke about how the family, including their young daughter, Camera, would deal with the situation.

and can exist without the fear of contracting the virus.

By creating this book together as a family, the Ashes were able to work with their tragic situation for some purpose. And, in the end, Jeanne was able to provide a lasting memory of Arthur for both Camera and herself. Ashe died in 1993.

Care for the Dying

Hospital care can be very cold and impersonal. That's why it is important to many people who are dying to be in their own homes or in a warm, familiar setting. This gives them the opportunity to die with dignity, surrounded by the people who love them.

One alternative to hospital care for AIDS patients is hospice care. It can be less expensive than hospital care and a lot more comfortable.

The Hospice
Hospices provide a program of services in the hospital or at home for people who are dying, and for their families. A hospice team may include doctors, nurses, home-health aides, social workers, and chaplains. Hospice care provides psychological, social, and spiritual care as well as medical care.

Hospice care is designed to make patients feel comfortable, to control their pain, and to provide them with proper nutrition. Home care programs usually require that there be a primary support system such as a partner, family, or friends to help in the home. The hospice worker may feed and bathe the patient, take care of personal hygiene, change the bed sheets, and do other necessary services for the person with the illness. Unlike hospital care, most hospice care will not include treating new complications of an illness or offering any extraordinary care to resuscitate—to keep alive—a person nearing death. The programs usually provide services for people with a life expectancy of six months or less.

Celebrate a Life

When someone dies, our sadness tends to make us forget about the life the person led before he or she became sick. But we have to change our way of thinking from mourning a death to celebrating a life. We need to talk about a person's accomplishments and contributions, the way he or she affected others, brought joy to people, or participated in simple daily life. Sometimes this is done at a funeral, and sometimes it's done at a later time in a memorial service, away from hospitals, funeral homes, and cemeteries. This is a healthy way to say good-bye to someone you cared about and to help you move on in your own life.

CHAPTER 7

AIDS Is Everyone's Problem

Q My name is Devon. The other day I overheard a lady saying that she wasn't worried about AIDS, because she didn't know anyone who had it. And that only certain kinds of people have it. Is this true? I thought there was an AIDS epidemic in the United States.

A Because AIDS comes from intimate contact, and because the initial infection is invisible, sometimes HIV seems to be limited to certain groups or certain areas of the United States. And while it is true that certain behavior will make it more likely for you to be infected with HIV, it is a disease that can touch anyone's life. It doesn't discriminate against race or religion; it doesn't matter whether you're male or female, gay or straight, rich or poor. We are all at risk; we are all living with AIDS. And, yes, there is an AIDS epidemic.

• • • • • • • • • • •

There are certain communities of people who have been hit harder by the AIDS virus. But this does not mean that AIDS only affects these people. This kind of thinking is what caused so much time to go by before more was done about AIDS.

For example, when the AIDS epidemic was first discovered, most of the people who were infected were homosexual men. This community has been hit so hard that it is not unusual for people to have had 25 or more friends die of the disease. However, currently the number of cases in the homosexual community is decreasing.

So it's incorrect to believe that all gay people have or will get AIDS. In fact, in San Francisco, the first city struck by the disease, the number of new cases has dropped by 50 percent. This is mainly due to effective prevention programs that get the word out about how HIV is transmitted. But this doesn't mean there's nothing to worry about. Safer sex practices need to continue, particularly among young, homosexual men.

Other statistics are proving that AIDS is not a disease that only targets some groups. The numbers are rising among heterosexual men and women, IV drug users, and both gay and heterosexual teenagers. Teens may think it can't happen to them, because they haven't often seen many other teens sick with the virus. This is because of the long time period that may occur between being infected with HIV and the appearance of full-blown AIDS. However, the CDC estimates that at least 40,000 new HIV infections occur each year among adolescents and adults. AIDS is the sixth leading cause of death for 15- to 25-year-olds.

While nearly half of infected women originally contracted HIV through contaminated needles, more and more are becoming infected through unprotected sex with infected men. AIDS is also increasing outside of big cities, in smaller towns and rural areas.

The Public's Response to AIDS

Most analysts do not believe that the U.S. government has provided enough leadership in helping the public respond to the health crisis caused by the HIV/AIDS epidemic. A brief review of what has happened and what has *not* happened in the country since AIDS was identified in 1981 may be helpful for you.

Tens of thousands of gay rights activists, many dying of AIDS, protest on the Mall in Washington, D.C., in October, 1987. Many spoke out against the government's slow response to the health crisis caused by the HIV/AIDS epidemic.

Federal Policies

Only in 1990 did Congress enact the first federal legislation providing care for persons with HIV and AIDS. Emergency relief was provided to fund prevention, health services, and health care in communities hardest hit by AIDS, and housing options for the homeless were covered. However, funding was low, and there is no coordinated federal policy for HIV/AIDS research, prevention, or care. While persons with HIV were included among those protected by the 1990 Americans with Disabilities Act, many federal programs still continue to discriminate against persons with HIV/AIDS, especially in HIV testing programs.

State and Local Policies

State and local governments, therefore, have most of the responsibility for the health care of persons with HIV/AIDS, but there has been little legislative and public support for adequate funding. Without federal monies, local governments have often been paralyzed or slow to provide care.

Other Institutions

Religious institutions have helped enormously in providing care for persons with AIDS-related illnesses, but they have been unable or sometimes unwilling to influence public policies in support of containing the AIDS crisis. Newspapers, magazines, and television prefer to tell the stories of certain infected public figures or cover sensational events rather than examine the plight of all the thousands of other people with HIV/AIDS.

Ordinary People

Ordinary people with AIDS have become the most active advocates for the development of appropriate public policies. They have become self-educated and have taken a great role in managing their own health. Unfortunately, many of these people who live far from the centers of information and support are not able to achieve notable results on their own behalf.

A Lasting Legacy
One notable effort to arouse public awareness about AIDS is the AIDS Memorial Quilt. The project was created in 1987 by Cleve Jones in San Francisco as a memorial to a friend. Each square or panel of the quilt represents a person who has died of AIDS. The panels are each three feet by six feet—the size of a human grave. Each panel is designed by friends, family, loved ones, and co-workers. Each is uniquely decorated with personal mementos, such as jewelry, sequins, teddy bears, pieces of clothing, and photographs. The quilt was last displayed in 1992 in Washington, D.C., on the Capitol mall. It covered an area larger than 16 football fields, or 18 acres. At last count, the quilt contained some 26,613 panels and weighed 31 tons.

The AIDS Memorial Quilt project traveled around the country to awaken people to the AIDS crisis. The giant quilt commemorating those who have died of AIDS was displayed in Denver in April, 1988. Many visitors were moved to tears.

The quilt is maintained by an organization called The NAMES Project, and during public displays, donation bins are put out to encourage contributions for AIDS-related causes. Sections of the quilt are displayed in high school and university programs throughout the country. There are 39 chapters of The NAMES Project in the United States and 27 international chapters.

An event called "Day Without Art" took place on December 1, 1989, and has been repeated on that day annually. Intended to raise public consciousness about AIDS, it was orga-

A marcher in a gay rights parade in New York City in 1992 reaches out to everybody with his sign.

nized by Visual AIDS, an organization of New York City artists and professionals as part of the World Health Organization's AIDS Awareness Day. As a way of mourning the many people who have been lost to the world of art through AIDS, galleries and museums shroud or remove works of art for the day, musicians and actors stop performing in the midst of their pieces, and buildings—including the White House in Washington, D.C.—in cities around the world shut off illuminating floodlights for a period of time at night. In addition, those who observe this day dress completely in black and wear a red ribbon—the well-known symbol for AIDS. Many high schools and colleges have also participated in events that observe this day.

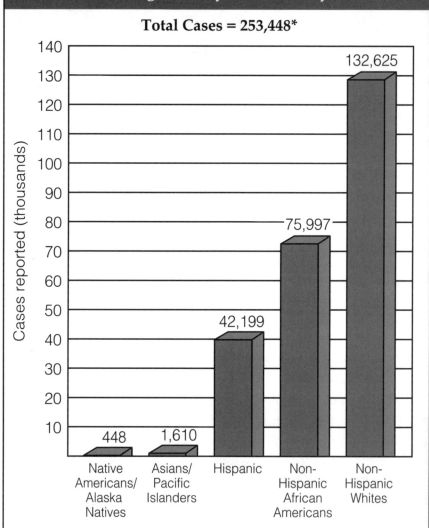

AIDS Cases Reported to Centers for Disease Control (CDC) Through 1992, by Race/Ethnicity

Total Cases = 253,448*

Cases reported (thousands)

- Native Americans/ Alaska Natives: 448
- Asians/ Pacific Islanders: 1,610
- Hispanic: 42,199
- Non-Hispanic African Americans: 75,997
- Non-Hispanic Whites: 132,625

*Includes 569 persons of unknown race/ethnicity.
Source: *Surgeon General's Report to the American Public on HIV Infection and AIDS*, Centers for Disease Control and Prevention (CDC), Health Resources and Services Administration, National Institutes of Health, June 1993.

Health Care Policies

Because of President Bill Clinton's introduction of major health care reform, there is much discussion of health care in the United States today. It usually points to the failure of the present system to meet the needs of all citizens, especially those with AIDS.

■ Many persons with AIDS cannot pay for health care, and the rise in the total number of people with AIDS spells out disaster for the future unless there is a change in policy.

■ The federally funded Medicaid system does not supply care to all of the poor and disabled, and private insurance plans often refuse to cover persons with AIDS.

■ Medical research on AIDS has been criticized for both the amount spent and the focus of the research, and the approval process has come under debate.

Judgmental attitudes, fear, and prejudice have often blocked the distribution of educational materials and equipment to prevent the spread of AIDS. Funds have not been raised, and the resulting lack of both knowledge and preventive measures has contributed to a tragic rise in HIV cases. Until the country steps up its level of concern and involvement in these issues, the AIDS epidemic will continue to grow.

AIDS and You

Although general awareness and concern about AIDS have grown only slowly, because the disease is affecting so many young people in the prime of their life, our whole society is changing. AIDS is changing the way we deal with relationships—physically, socially, and emotionally. Most people are beginning to realize that engaging in risky behaviors could mean the difference between life or death. This doesn't mean your teenage years have to come to a grinding halt. But you need to come to terms with the existence of AIDS and make some responsible decisions about your life.

What You Can Do
Here is a checklist of questions you might ask yourself while making these decisions:

■ Have I educated myself thoroughly about AIDS?

■ Do I understand the consequences for myself and others if I engage in risky behavior?

■ How much do I care about the welfare of my generation? Have I truly dealt with the fact that many of us are dying?

■ Can I commit myself to help in the battle against the spread of AIDS, and how may I best take part?

Many teens have already begun to do their part in the fight against AIDS. They have begun to talk freely and honestly about AIDS to one another. They are reacting against fear and ignorance about the disease and are educating one another. They have started support groups and hot line numbers; they have had fund-raisers and written letters to the President or to Congress about getting more funding for AIDS research and health care.

Most of all, teenagers today are becoming supportive and caring toward people with AIDS. They have taken the first step toward recognizing the human cost of the disease. As tomorrow's leaders of society, they are learning about the importance of taking stands and making choices. Follow their lead, and make sure your choice is for life.

Where to Go for Help

There are several organizations and hot line numbers you can call to find out more information about AIDS and disease prevention.

United States

National AIDS Hotline
(800) 342-AIDS (2437)

National AIDS Hotline in
Spanish
(800) 344-SIDA (7432)

National AIDS Hotline for the
Hearing Impaired
(800) 243-7889

CDC National AIDS
Clearinghouse
P.O. Box 6003
Rockville, MD 20849-6003
(800) 458-5231

National Sexually Transmitted
Disease Hotline
(800) 227-8922

Youth Crisis Hotline
(800) HIT-HOME

National Teen AIDS Hotline
(800) 234-TEEN (8336)

National Gay/Lesbian Hotline
(800) 221-7044

National Minority AIDS Council
(202) 544-1076

Hemophilia Foundation
(212) 682-5510 (You may call
collect.)

Planned Parenthood Federation
of America
(212) 541-7800

National Council of Churches
(NCC)
AIDS Task Force
(212) 870-2385

Canada

The AIDS Committee of Ottawa
267 Dalhousie St.
Ottawa, ON KIN 7E3
(613) 238-5014
Hotline: (613) 238-4111

AIDS Committee of Toronto
(ACT)
P.O. Box 55, Station F
Toronto, ON MAY 2L4
(416) 926-0063
Hotline: (416) 926-1626

Comite SIDA Aide Montreal
(CSAM)
3600, avenue Hôtel-de-Ville
Montreal, PQ H2X 3B6
(514) 282-9888

For More Information

Books

Barlett, John G. *The Guide to Living with HIV Infection.* Johns Hopkins, 1991.

Blake, Jeanne. *Risky Times, A Guide for Teenagers.* Workman, 1990.

Draimin, Barbara Hermie, DSW. *Coping When a Parent Has AIDS.* Rosen, 1993.

Flanders, Stephen A., and Carl N. Flanders. *AIDS.* Facts On File, 1990.

Ford, Michael Thomas. *100 Questions and Answers About AIDS, A Guide for Young People.* Macmillan, 1992.

Foster, Carol D., et al., eds. *AIDS.* Info Plus TX, 1992.

Froman, Paul Kent. *After You Say Goodbye.* Chronicle, 1992.

Johnson, Anthony G. *Rock and a Hard Place.* Crown, 1993.

Johnson, Earvin "Magic." *What You Can Do to Avoid AIDS.* Times Books, 1992.

Kittredge, Mary. *Teens with AIDS Speak Out.* Silver Burdett, 1990.

Shilts, Randy. *And the Band Played On: Politics, People and the AIDS Epidemic.* St. Martin's, 1987.

Silverstein, Alvin, and Virginia B. Silverstein, eds. *AIDS: Deadly Threat.* Enslow, 1991.

Sirimarco, Elizabeth. *AIDS.* Marshall Cavendish, 1993.

White, Ryan, and Anne Marie Cunningham. *Ryan White: My Own Story.* Dial, 1991.

Publications

AIDS Medical Guide. San Francisco AIDS Foundation, 1992.

Fact Sheets. Centers for Disease Control and Prevention (CDC) Division of HIV/AIDS, 1993.

Positively Aware (quarterly journal). Test Positive Aware Network, Inc., 1993.

Surgeon General's Report to the American Public on HIV Infection and AIDS. Centers for Disease Control and Prevention (CDC), Health, 1993.

Videos

Answers About Aids. American Red Cross, 1987.

Til Death Do Us Part. Durrin Films/New Day Films, 1748 Kalorama Road NW, Washington, D.C. 20009, 1988.

What Is AIDS? Coronet/MTI Film & Video, 108 Wilmot Road, Deerfield, IL 60015, 1988.

INDEX

616.97   Lerman-Golomb,
LER   Barbara.

          AIDS.

                              36403000021604
$24.26

DATE			